Izzy Gizmo

Written by Pip Jones
Illustrated by Sara Ogilvie

PEACHTREE
ATLANTA

IZZY GIZMO, a girl who loved to invent,
carried her tool bag wherever she went,
in case she discovered a thing to be mended
or a gadget to tweak to make it more splendid.

But the trouble with things that have dials and switches is they don't always work; they have certain glitches.

The **Tea-Mendous**, for instance, did such a fine job...

'til out popped a piston and off dropped a knob!

Then the **Swirly-Spagsonic** (for eating spaghetti) turned Grandpa's wallpaper into confetti.

The **Beard-Tastic** had Grandpa near perfectly styled...
'til the foam overflowed, and the clippers went wild.

Well, Izabelle, who was so clever and bright,
would get rather cross when things didn't go right.
And she huffed, "It's too tough! I've had it! I quit."

She kicked her invention
and called it a "twit!"

Izabelle fumed.

Grandpa smiled and chuckled.

"You can't just quit 'cos that thingy-bob buckled.
Now, trust me, young lady. Sometimes you need
to try again and again if you want to succeed."

Perhaps Grandpa was right, but still, Izabelle sighed.
She picked up her tool bag and wandered outside.

Kicking the stones on the path as she walked,
Izzy jumped at a bump!
Up ahead, something squawked.

From the clouds,
a poor crow had taken

a tumble,

and landed—

KAPOOOOF!

—in a feathery
jumble.

Izzy ran to the vet's. But he just shook his head.
"His wing is too broken to fix," the doc said.
"Perhaps take him home, and there you could try
to teach him to live as a crow who can't fly."

Day after day, Izzy thought she had found
something fun for her crow to do on the ground.

Like digging for worms,

and racing fat slugs,

hopscotch and hoopla,

and searching for bugs.

But the heartbroken crow simply gazed at the sky,
as the other birds sang and flew happily by.

One night, with the crow in the folds of her sweater,
Izzy sighed, "Oh, I wish I could make him feel better.

I've tried.
He won't play.
He won't drink.
He won't eat."

She was so very close
to admitting defeat.

Grandpa said, "Izzy! Don't give up on him now.
I know you can do it. Just work out how!"

Then Grandpa passed Izzy her gadgety things,

and she knew what to do!
"I'll invent some
new wings!"

Izzy piled up her books, and she started to read,

then she made a long list of the things she would need.

She searched for some batteries and old electronics,
dismantled a mixer and the **Swirly-Spagsonic**.

The crow watched, entranced, and he held Izzy's drill,
while she bent, bashed and battered, and walloped until—

"Ta-Da!"

Izzy fastened the wings with a strap,

but they hummed and they twitched, far too heavy to flap.

"AAARRGGHHH!"

Izzy yelled. "I'm no good at succeeding!"
The crow softly cawed,
his beady eyes pleading.

"What now?" Izzy cried.
"Try again," Grandpa said.

"Okay, follow me!"
And with that, off she sped.

Izzy dove in a pond, where she borrowed a pump.

Then she took from an engine
two sprockets, a sump.

Izzy fastened the wings.
They were light.
They were curvy.

But the wings, the wrong shape,
turned the crow

topsy-turvy!

"I give up!"

Izzy yelled,
with a furious frown.

The crow sadly cawed,
as he hung upside down.

Izzy unscrewed the head from the shower,

found special circuits,
to adjust the wings' power,

and finally, using her trusty old pliers,
she borrowed the motors from two big blow-dryers.

"Yes!" Izzy said. "The right shape, perfect weight..."

But one wing flapped madly.

The crow couldn't fly straight.

"I've had it!" yelled Izzy, heading straight for a bin.
But the crow blocked her path. He just wouldn't give in.

Izzy twizzled and tinkered, and, using his beak,
the tip-tapping crow gave the screws a good tweak
Then he loosened the cog from Grandpa's old mixer—

"You can fly!"

Izzy cried.

"Oh! Your name should be

Fixer!"

After two

loop

the

loops,

Fixer came into land,

and stood, happily cawing, upon Izzy's hand.
"You tried very hard," Grandpa said, "and succeeded!
You kept at it, Izzy. You did what was needed."

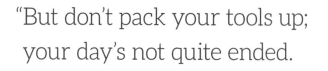
"But don't pack your tools up;
  your day's not quite ended.

A few things around here now need to be mended!"

For Isabella Grace and Isabelle Bee xx —P. J.

For Sita, Dani, and Holger —S. O.

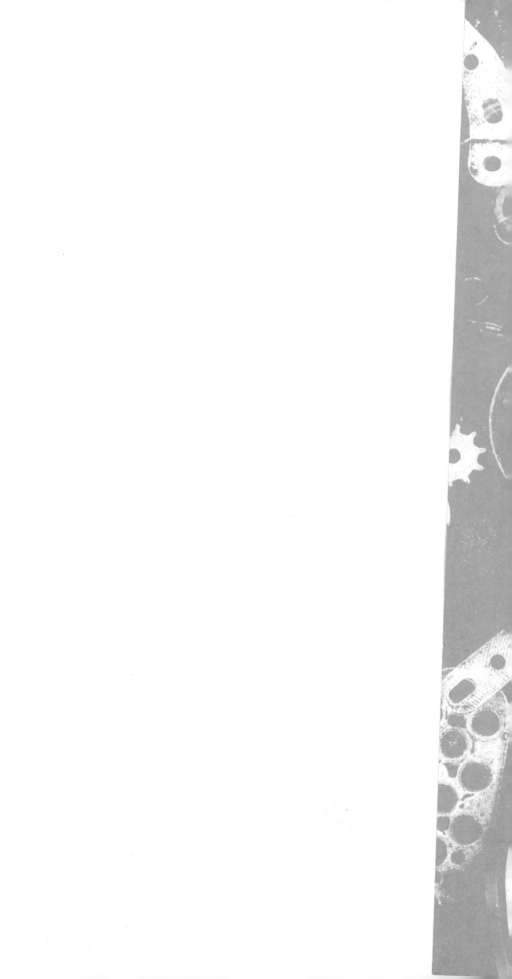

Published by
Peachtree Publishers
1700 Chattahoochee Avenue
Atlanta, Georgia 30318-2112
www.peachtree-online.com

Text © 2017 by Pip Jones
Illustrations © 2017 by Sara Ogilvie

First published in Great Britain in 2011 by Simon & Schuster UK Ltd
1St Floor, 222 Gray's Inn Road, London, WC1X 8HB
A CBS Company.
First United States version published in 2018 by Peachtree Publishers

The illustrations were created in pencil, ink, oil pastel, monoprint and digital techniques.

Printed in September 2017 in China
10 9 8 7 6 5 4 3 2 1
First Edition

HC: 978-1-68263-021-1

Library of Congress Cataloging-in-Publication Data

Names: Jones, Pip (Children's story writer), author. | Ogilvie, Sara,
1971– illustrator.
Title: Izzy Gizmo / written by Pip Jones ; illustrated by Sara Ogilvie.
Description: First edition. | Atlanta : Peachtree Publishers, 2018. |
Summary: Izzy Gizmo loves to invent but gets frustrated when her
inventions fail to work properly, so when she finds a crow with a broken
wing her grandfather urges her to persist until she finds a way to help.
Identifiers: LCCN 2017017494 | ISBN 9781682630211
Subjects: | CYAC: Stories in rhyme. | Inventors—Fiction. | Perseverance
(Ethics)—Fiction. | Animal rescue—Fiction. | Grandfathers—Fiction.
Classification: LCC PZ8.3.J75365 Iz 2018 | DDC [E]—dc23 LC record available
at https://lccn.loc.gov/2017017494

A few things around here now need to be mended!"

For Isabella Grace and Isabelle Bee xx —P. J.

For Sita, Dani, and Holger —S. O.

Published by
Peachtree Publishers
1700 Chattahoochee Avenue
Atlanta, Georgia 30318-2112
www.peachtree-online.com

Text © 2017 by Pip Jones
Illustrations © 2017 by Sara Ogilvie

First published in Great Britain in 2011 by Simon & Schuster UK Ltd
1St Floor, 222 Gray's Inn Road, London, WC1X 8HB
A CBS Company.
First United States version published in 2018 by Peachtree Publishers

The illustrations were created in pencil, ink, oil pastel, monoprint and digital techniques.

Printed in September 2017 in China
10 9 8 7 6 5 4 3 2 1
First Edition

HC: 978-1-68263-021-1

Library of Congress Cataloging-in-Publication Data

Names: Jones, Pip (Children's story writer), author. | Ogilvie, Sara, 1971– illustrator.
Title: Izzy Gizmo / written by Pip Jones ; illustrated by Sara Ogilvie.
Description: First edition. | Atlanta : Peachtree Publishers, 2018. |
Summary: Izzy Gizmo loves to invent but gets frustrated when her inventions fail to work properly, so when she finds a crow with a broken wing her grandfather urges her to persist until she finds a way to help.
Identifiers: LCCN 2017017494 | ISBN 9781682630211
Subjects: | CYAC: Stories in rhyme. | Inventors—Fiction. | Perseverance (Ethics)—Fiction. | Animal rescue—Fiction. | Grandfathers—Fiction.
Classification: LCC PZ8.3.J75365 Iz 2018 | DDC [E]—dc23 LC record available at https://lccn.loc.gov/2017017494